W9-APC-446

Pirates

C. Drew Lamm
illustrated by Stacey Schuett

Hyperion Books for Children

New York

Text copyright © 2001 by C. Drew Lamm
Illustrations copyright © 2001 by Stacey Schuett
All rights reserved. No part of this book may be reproduced or transmitted in any form or by
any means, electronic or mechanical, including photocopying, recording, or by any information
storage and retrieval system, without written permission from the publisher.
For information address
Hyperion Books for Children, 114 Fifth Avenue, New York, New York 10011-5690.
Printed in Singapore
First Edition

1 3 5 7 9 10 8 6 4 2

Library of Congress Cataloging-in-Publication Data
Lamm, C. Drew.
Pirates/by C. Drew Lamm; illustrated by Stacey Schuett.—1st ed.
p.   cm.
Summary: When Ellery reads her younger brother a scary book about pirates,
Max finds an appropriate way to make her close the book.
ISBN 0-7868-0392-4 (hc)
[1. Pirates—Fiction. 2. Brothers and sisters—Fiction. 3. Books and reading—Fiction.
4. Fear—Fiction.] I. Schuett, Stacey, ill. II. Title.
PZ7.L181Pi 2000
[Fic]—dc21   98-52662

Visit www.hyperionchildrensbooks.com

3 9082 08622 5896

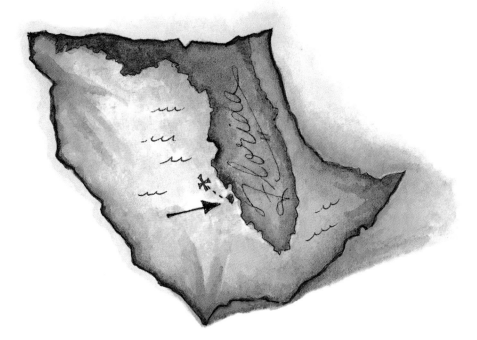

To Ellery Rose,
Carmen twice,
Cayo Costa Etienne,
and Lesley, who insists that Gaspar is her
great, great grandmother in disguise!
—D. L.

To Clare and Ian
—S. S.

Max grabbed Ellery's library bag.
"What did you bring?" he asked.
"Pirates," said Ellery.
"They aren't very nice," said Max.
"They're vicious," said Ellery.

"How about something else," said Max. "What about cats?"

"Pirates," said Ellery.

Max dumped the bag onto the floor. The book fell out.

On the cover stood a pirate. He had a black eye patch and held a silver sword that was plunged into the ground in front of him.

"Let's read it tomorrow morning," said Max.

"No," said Ellery, "tonight in the dark when we're alone."

WITHDRAWN

After the sun set and the day disappeared, Ellery led
Max down the hall, keeping close to the wall—down the
stairs, over the third step that creaked, and into the den.

Ellery pulled out the book and a flashlight. She
arranged her sleeping bag in the bay window. Max curled
up in the armchair.
In the dim and flickering light, Ellery began to read.

"By the Gulf of Mexico, on a deserted island, pirates count their gold. They creep in the night with loot hanging off their fingers. They bury treasure in the soft sand, scratch out maps with their jagged fingernails, and mark X on the spot where they'll dig again.

"Australian pines form a windbreak guarding the island from the lash of storms. Spanish moss hangs from the trees."

"Like green tinsel," said Max.
"Pirate's hair," said Ellery.
Max dragged his sleeping bag over to the window seat and peered at the pictures.
"This is too scary," said Max. "Let's get another book."

"Across the channel stands the island of Gasparilla. The wicked pirate José Gaspar sails his pirate ship through these waters. He loots ships that hold treasure and murders anyone who tries to hold on to their gold. He ruled these waters a long, long, not so long time ago.

"Gaspar picks his teeth with the bones of shipmates. He tears treasures from quivering girls' necks and yanks gold from old men's molars," said Ellery.

"He buries his treasures in . . ."

"Treasure chests," guessed Max.
"Coffins," said Ellery.

". . . in chests full of . . ."

"Coins, silver, and gold," said Max hopefully.
"Diamond and ruby rings still attached to fingers," said Ellery.

"On the edge of the island, bushes squat in the mud of a mishmash marsh where stamping alligators live. They know where treasure is hidden. They sharpen their teeth on treasure hunters digging for . . ."

"Rubies and emeralds and gold," said Max.
"Skulls and skeletons and blood," said Ellery.

"Crows glisten. Their feathers shine, their black eyes
bright. They pierce the skies with their cries at night."

"Noisy crows," said Max, trying to think of something other than pirates.
"They're pirates turned into crows by a sorcerer whose ship they tried to loot,"
said Ellery, turning the page.

"On stormy nights, gold and silver are strewn along the beach from pirate ships."

"Maybe their treasures turn to shells. If you shake a handful of shells, you hear the clink of silver," said Max.

"If you shake two handfuls, you hear the shudder of skeleton maidens," said Ellery.

"Orange-edged sea stars slide toward the ocean—stars stolen from the galaxies by pirate ships. Ghost crabs watch from sand tunnels with telescope eyes."

"They watch for the tide," said Max.
"They watch for pirates returning on stormy nights," said Ellery.

Max looked out the window. "It might rain."
He quivered. "Let's read something else."
"Thunder'll probably crack the house open," said Ellery.

"Perched on their pier, ancient pelicans thrust their heads up into the rain. They turn their heads inside out with their gaping mouths."

"They stretch to catch raindrops," said Max.
"They scream silent screams of pirate victims," said Ellery.

The night grew deep dark. The pirate book slid on Ellery's knees. Max pulled his sleeping bag over his head and breathed lightly into its darkness. He shivered.

"That piece of cloth tied on the pirate's head is a murdered captain's shirt," said Ellery.

Max shivered again. He drew his knees up to his chin. "It's raining wicked tonight," he whispered.

Ellery sat straight up, her eyes wide.

"Max, listen. A pirate. I hear his walk. He's coming closer, closer. . . ."

They smelled his salt breath. They heard his wooden leg . . . *thump, thup-thump, thup-thump* . . . and felt his long filthy nails . . . *scratch, scrat-scratch, scrat-scratch* . . . against the windowpane.

Rain hit the window hard and fast. Branches scraped the glass. The sky shot light and slammed it into the ground. *BOOM!* Thunder.

Lightning flashed. The flashlight faltered, wavered, and died.

"Max? Max?"

Ellery gasped.

The room creaked in the wind and the wind blew and the room creaked like a pirate ship. It smelled sour. Dark pirate breath.

Pirates crept forward in search of silver fillings. Pirate shadows mumbled in low breaths and dug dirt-lined fingers under their eye patches. They rubbed their scarred eyes. They sneered and squinted like snakes staring into a setting sun.

"Max?"

Wind shook the windows. Sour breaths blew. Blew deep into their sleeping bags, blew under their skin. The pages in the book fluttered.

"Max?" called Ellery. "Max? Max!" she cried again.

"I think I read too far."

"CLOSE THE BOOK," said the pirate Gaspar.

Out of the deep, black night a hook clawed
Ellery's arm. It pulled. And pulled.
It yanked the book out of Ellery's hands.
Ellery screamed.
Something rattled. Something clattered.

"I'd rather read about cats," said Max.
And Ellery said, "Me, too!"

WITHDRAWN

The end

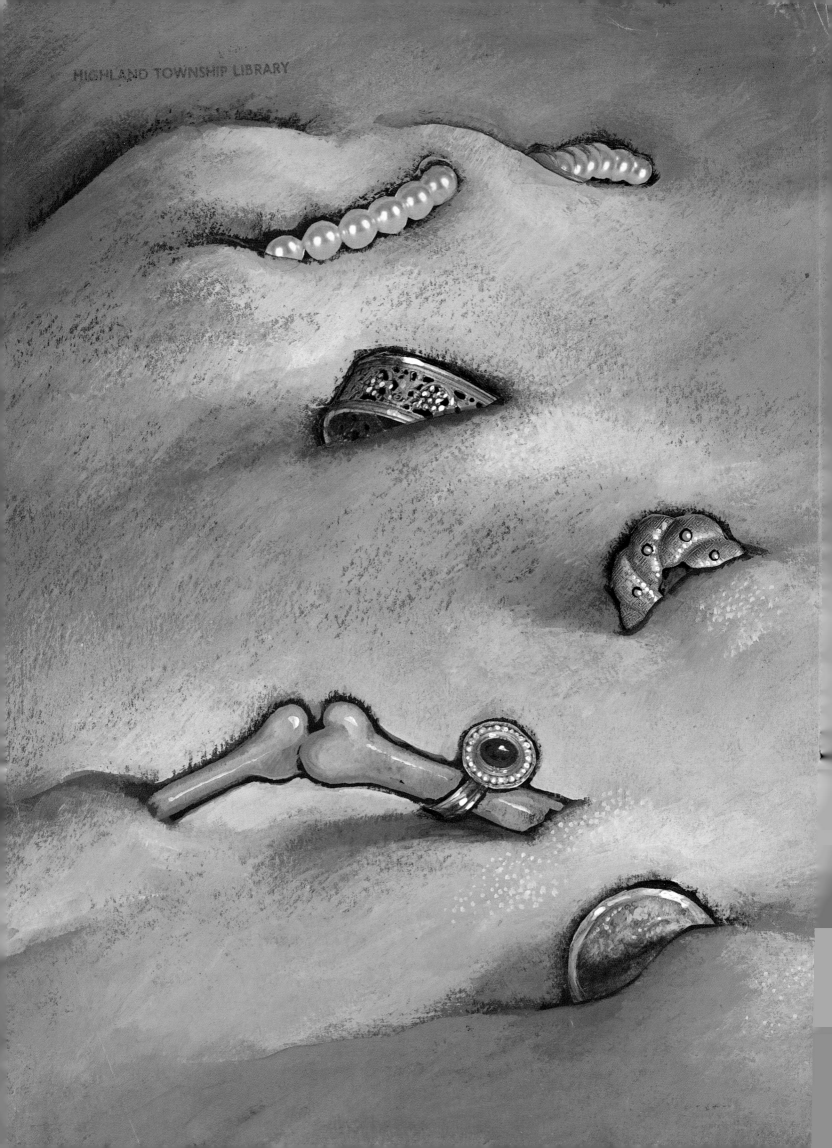
HIGHLAND TOWNSHIP LIBRARY